W9-AGJ-716

Dear Parents:

Congratulations! Your child is taking the first steps on an exciting journey. The destination? Independent reading!

STEP INTO READING® will help your child get there. The program offers five steps to reading success. Each step includes fun stories and colorful art or photographs. In addition to original fiction and books with favorite characters, there are Step into Reading Non-Fiction Readers, Phonics Readers and Boxed Sets, Sticker Readers, and Comic Readers—a complete literacy program with something to interest every child.

Learning to Read, Step by Step!

Ready to Read **Preschool–Kindergarten**
- big type and easy words • rhyme and rhythm • picture clues

For children who know the alphabet and are eager to begin reading.

Reading with Help **Preschool–Grade 1**
- basic vocabulary • short sentences • simple stories

For children who recognize familiar words and sound out new words with help.

Reading on Your Own **Grades 1–3**
- engaging characters • easy-to-follow plots • popular topics

For children who are ready to read on their own.

Reading Paragraphs **Grades 2–3**
- challenging vocabulary • short paragraphs • exciting stories

For newly independent readers who read simple sentences with confidence.

Ready for Chapters **Grades 2–4**
- chapters • longer paragraphs • full-color art

For children who want to take the plunge into chapter books but still like colorful pictures.

STEP INTO READING® is designed to give every child a successful reading experience. The grade levels are only guides; children will progress through the steps at their own speed, developing confidence in their reading.

Remember, a lifetime love of reading starts with a single step!

Disney · PIXAR

SUPER STORY COLLECTION

Published in the United States by Random House Children's Books, a division of Penguin Random House LLC, 1745 Broadway, New York, NY 10019, and in Canada by Penguin Random House Canada Limited, Toronto, in conjunction with Disney Enterprises, Inc.

Originally published as *Ocean of Color,* copyright © 2016 Disney Enterprises, Inc. and Pixar Animation Studios; *Crash, Boom, Roar!,* copyright © 2015 Disney Enterprises, Inc. and Pixar Animation Studios; *Just Keep Swimming,* copyright © 2005 Disney Enterprises, Inc. and Pixar Animation Studios; *Mom, Dad, and Me,* copyright © 2016 Disney Enterprises, Inc. and Pixar Animation Studios; *The Journey Home,* copyright © 2015 Disney Enterprises, Inc. and Pixar Animation Studios; *Dory's Story,* copyright © 2016 Disney Enterprises, Inc. and Pixar Animation Studios; and *Journey into the Mind,* copyright © 2015 Disney Enterprises, Inc. and Pixar Animation Studios. All rights reserved.

Visit us on the Web!
StepIntoReading.com
randomhousekids.com

Educators and librarians, for a variety of teaching tools, visit us at RHTeachersLibrarians.com

ISBN 978-0-7364-3672-4

Printed in the United States of America 10 9 8 7 6 5 4 3 2

7 Early Readers!

STEP INTO READING®

Disney·PIXAR

SUPER STORY COLLECTION

With Poster and Over 30 Stickers!

Step 1, 2, and 3 Books

A Collection of Seven Early Readers

Random House New York

Contents

Ocean of Color 9

Crash, Boom, Roar! . . . 33

Just Keep Swimming 57

Mom, Dad, and Me . . . 89

The Journey Home 113

Dory's Story 137

Journey into the Mind 161

STEP INTO READING®

OCEAN OF COLOR

by Bill Scollon

illustrated by the Disney Storybook Art Team

Random House New York

Dory is a blue fish
who lives in the sea.

Marlin and Nemo

are orange fish.

Dory remembers
her mom and dad!

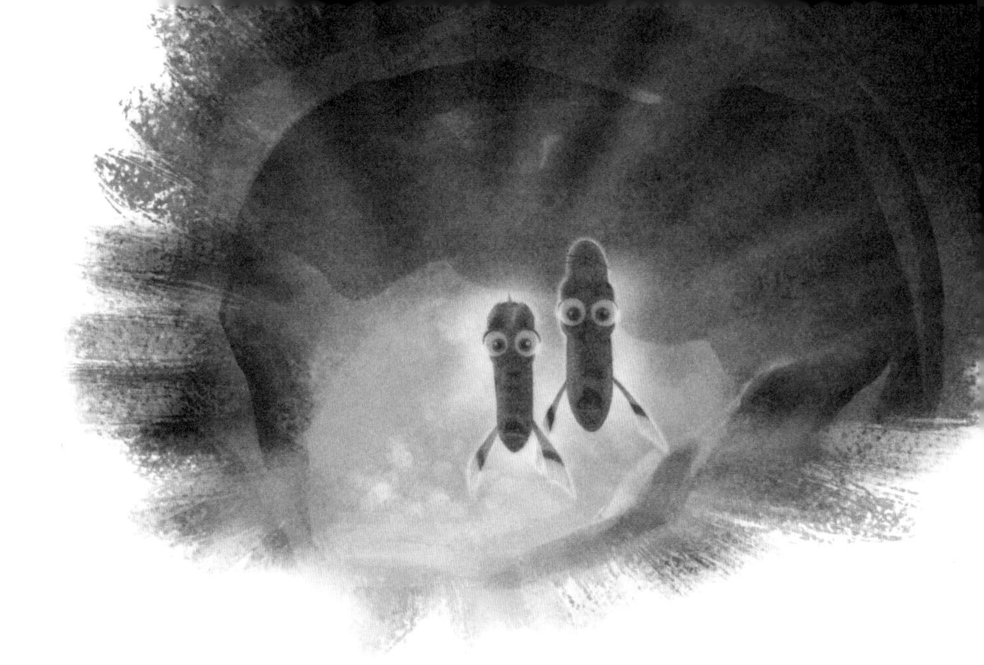

They are blue,
like Dory.

Dory swims
into the deep,
dark ocean.

She wants to find
her mom and dad.

Dory meets Hank.

He is red.

Bailey is a beluga whale.

He is white.

Destiny is a whale shark.

She has white spots.

The otter is brown.

He loves to cuddle.

Becky is a loon.
Her feathers are black,
blue, and white.

Dory sees a

purple sea urchin.

Dory finds many fish.
They are lots of colors.

Dory spies some pink coral.

She is home!

Dory sees yellow fish.
She does not see
her mom and dad.

Dory swims through
the green kelp.

Dory sees two fish.

They are blue, like Dory.

Dory finds

her mom and dad!

Dory loves her colorful
family and friends!

Disney · PIXAR

THE GOOD DINOSAUR

CRASH, BOOM, ROAR!

by Susan Amerikaner

illustrated by the Disney Storybook Art Team

Random House New York

Poppa hears a sound.

What is it?

Crack. Crack! CRACK!

It is Arlo!

Arlo hears the river.

Burble. Bubble. Gurgle!

Arlo hears a storm.

Crash. Boom. Bang!

Spot and Arlo howl.

Yoooooowwww!

Arlo and Spot play.

Animals pop up.

Pop. Pop! POP!

A T. rex <u>ROARS</u>!

Spot bites.

Arlo yells.

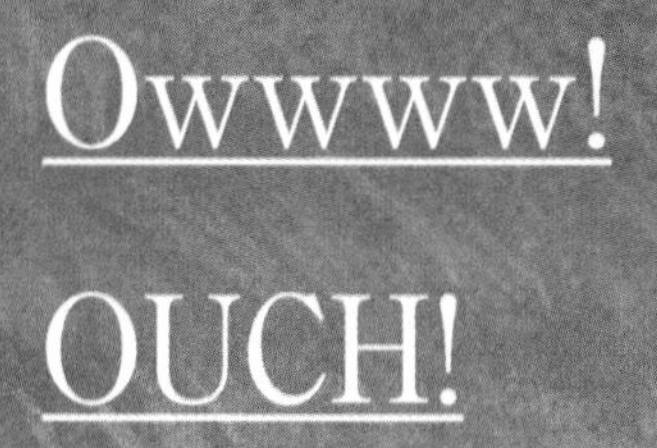

Owwww!

OUCH!

Arlo hears a fire.

Hiss. Crackle. Snap!

Arlo hears Momma.

ARLO!

Momma hears Arlo.

MOMMA!

The sound of home
is the best sound of all!

STEP INTO READING®

by Melissa Lagonegro
illustrated by Atelier Philippe Harchy

Random House New York

Nemo has a dream.
He wants to join
the school swim team.

But Nemo has
a little fin.

He thinks that

he will never win.

Dory helps Nemo.

She teaches him

to go, go, go!

Nemo races and races.

Nemo chases and chases.

"Just keep swimming,"
Dory sings.

But Nemo thinks
of other things.

“I will never win.
I have a bad fin.”

"Just keep swimming!"
Dory cries.

So Nemo tries . . .

and tries . . .

. . . and tries.

Nemo races and races.

Nemo chases and chases.

Yippee! Yahoo!

His dream comes true.

Nemo makes the team.

Can Nemo win the first-place prize?

“Just keep swimming!”
Dory cries.

Watch him race.

Watch him chase.

Watch as Nemo wins first place!

STEP INTO READING®

MOM, DAD, AND ME

by Christy Webster

Random House New York

This is Riley.
She lives with
her mom and dad
in a small town.

Mom and Dad take
good care of Riley.
They all love each
other very much.

Mom is smart and kind.

She gives the best hugs!

Dad is silly and fun.
He likes to play games.

Mom, Dad, and Riley
love their home.
There is a lake
near their house.

It is the perfect place
for Riley to grow up!

Riley, Mom, and Dad
love to play hockey.

© Disney/Pixar
© Disney/Pixar
© Disney/Pixar
© Disney/Pixar
© Disney/Pixar
© Disney/Pixar
© Disney/Pixar
© Disney/Pixar
© Disney/Pixar
© Disney/Pixar
© Disney/Pixar

© Disney/Pixar
© Disney/Pixar
© Disney/Pixar
© Disney/Pixar
© Disney/Pixar
© Disney/Pixar
© Disney/Pixar
© Disney/Pixar
© Disney/Pixar

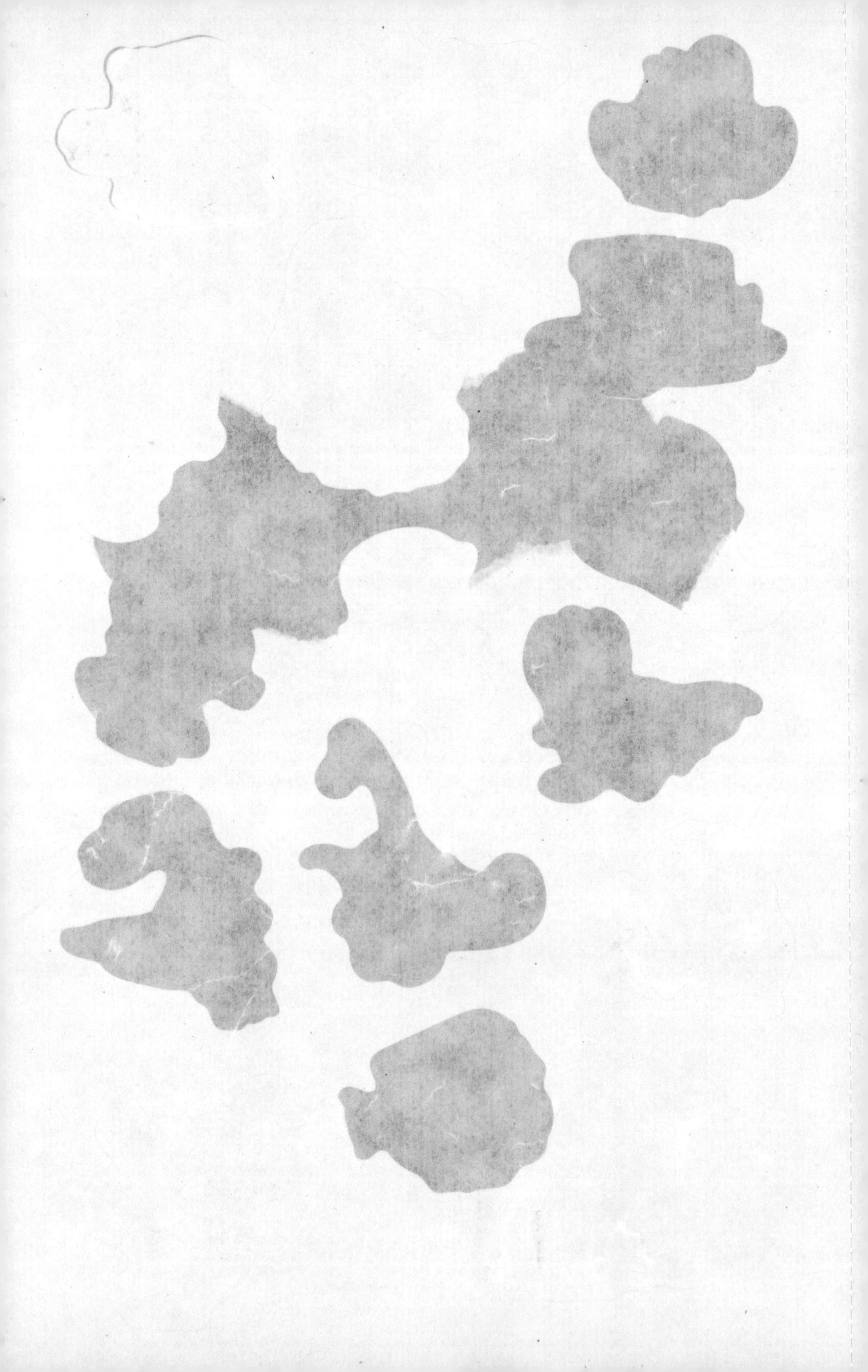

Hooray!

Riley scores a goal!

Riley has made
lots of memories
over the years.
Some are happy.

Some are sad.

Some are both!

One day,
Dad gets a new job
in a big city.

They sell their house
and move away.

Moving is hard
for Riley.
She is sad to leave
her old life behind.

The new house
is nothing
like the old one.
It does not feel
like home.

Riley goes
to a new school.
Will she make
new friends?

Mom has an idea.
She helps Riley join
a new hockey team!

Riley likes being
part of the team.
After a while,
she makes lots
of new friends.

Mom and Dad are
still her biggest fans.

Riley learns that
some things change.

But Mom and Dad will always be there for her.

Family is forever.

STEP INTO READING®

DISNEY · PIXAR

THE GOOD DINOSAUR

The Journey Home

by Bill Scollon
illustrated by the Disney Storybook Art Team

Random House New York

Arlo is a dinosaur.
He lives
with his family
on a farm.

Arlo is scared
of many things.
He is afraid
to leave the farm.

© Disney/Pixar

A wild boy steals food!

Arlo is scared.

He runs away.

Arlo and the boy
fall into the river.
The water sweeps
them away.

Arlo is far

from home.

The boy is gone.

Arlo is lost.

He is scared.

Arlo can follow the river

to get home.

The boy finds Arlo.
He brings food.
Arlo follows the boy
into the woods.

Arlo names the boy Spot.

They have fun together.

They become friends.

Arlo and Spot get lost.

They are attacked!

A pack of T. rexes
saves them.

Arlo and Spot are happy.
They will be home soon.

A human calls
to Spot.
Arlo is afraid that
Spot might leave.
But he stays with Arlo.

Arlo and Spot

are attacked again!

Spot is trapped

in a log.

This time,

Arlo is brave.

He fights

to help Spot.

A flash flood
is coming!
It almost carries
Spot away.

Arlo jumps
into the water.
He will save
his friend!

Arlo and Spot go
over a waterfall.
They swim to shore.
They are safe!

Spot meets a human family.
Arlo knows Spot should stay with them.
Arlo and Spot say goodbye.

Arlo is a brave dinosaur.
He finds the farm
on his own.
Arlo is home!

STEP INTO READING®

DORY'S STORY

by Bill Scollon
illustrated by the Disney Storybook Art Team

Random House New York

Dory is

a little fish.

She has trouble
with her memory.

Dory does not remember
how to get home.
She is lost.
She asks
everyone she
meets for help.

No one knows
where Dory lives.

Dory becomes friends
with Nemo and Marlin.
They all live together
in a coral reef.

One day, Dory remembers
a place called
the Jewel of Morro Bay.
Maybe her home is there!

Dory crosses the ocean
with Nemo and Marlin
to find her home.
She gets stuck
in a plastic ring!

Dory gets taken to
the Jewel of Morro Bay.
It is a big aquarium!

Nemo and Marlin
want to find Dory.
A bird carries them
into the aquarium!

Dory meets an octopus.
His name is Hank.
He helps Dory figure out
where her parents live.

Dory finds her home.
Her parents are gone.
A crab says they went
to the hospital.

The pipes will take Dory
to the hospital.
Destiny is a whale shark.
Bailey is a beluga.
They show Dory the way.

Nemo and Marlin
find Dory in the pipe.
They swim off together
to find Dory's parents.

Dory's parents are not at the fish hospital.

Dory falls
down a drain!
The drain drops her
into the ocean.

Dory is alone.

She follows a shell path.

It leads her

to her parents!

Nemo and Marlin are
on a truck
with the hospital fish.
Dory will save them!

Becky helps rescue
Nemo and Marlin.
Dory is still
in the truck!

Hank scares
the truck driver away.
They drive off the pier
into the ocean!

The fish are happy
to return to the sea.
Destiny and Bailey
join them!

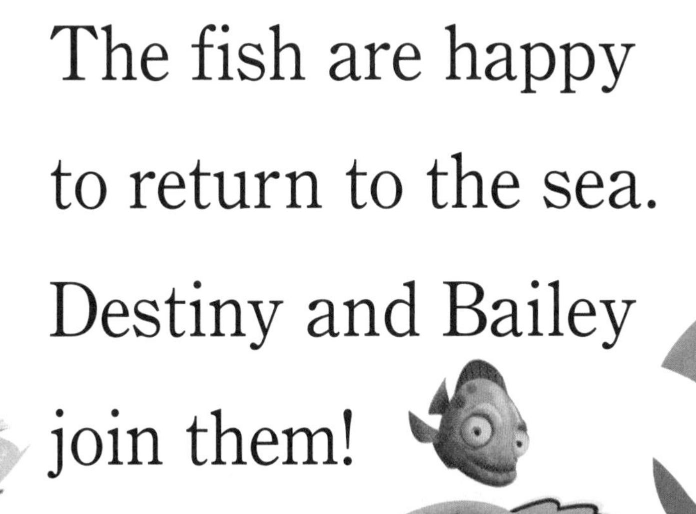

Dory's parents go

back to the reef

with Dory

and her friends.

They are all

one big happy family!

STEP INTO READING®

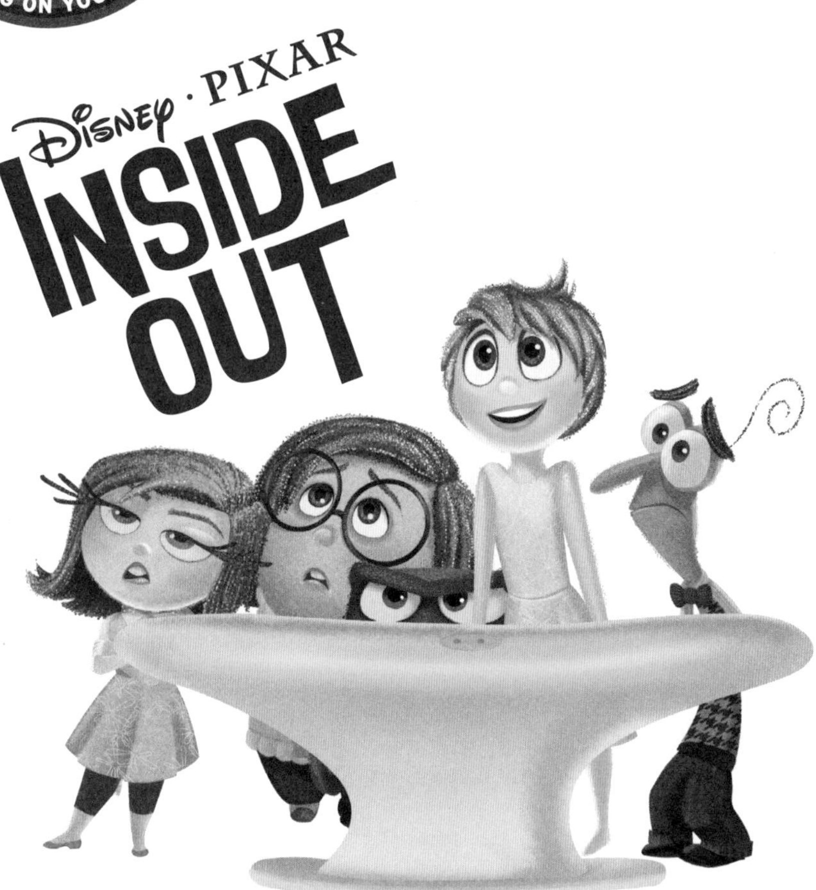

JOURNEY into the MIND

by Melissa Lagonegro

illustrated by the Disney Storybook Art Team

Random House New York

This is Headquarters.
It is in Riley's mind.
Riley is eleven years old.
Her mind is filled
with different Emotions.
They take care of her.

Joy is an Emotion.
Her job is
to keep Riley happy.
Joy wants Riley
to have happy core memories.
Happy memories are yellow.

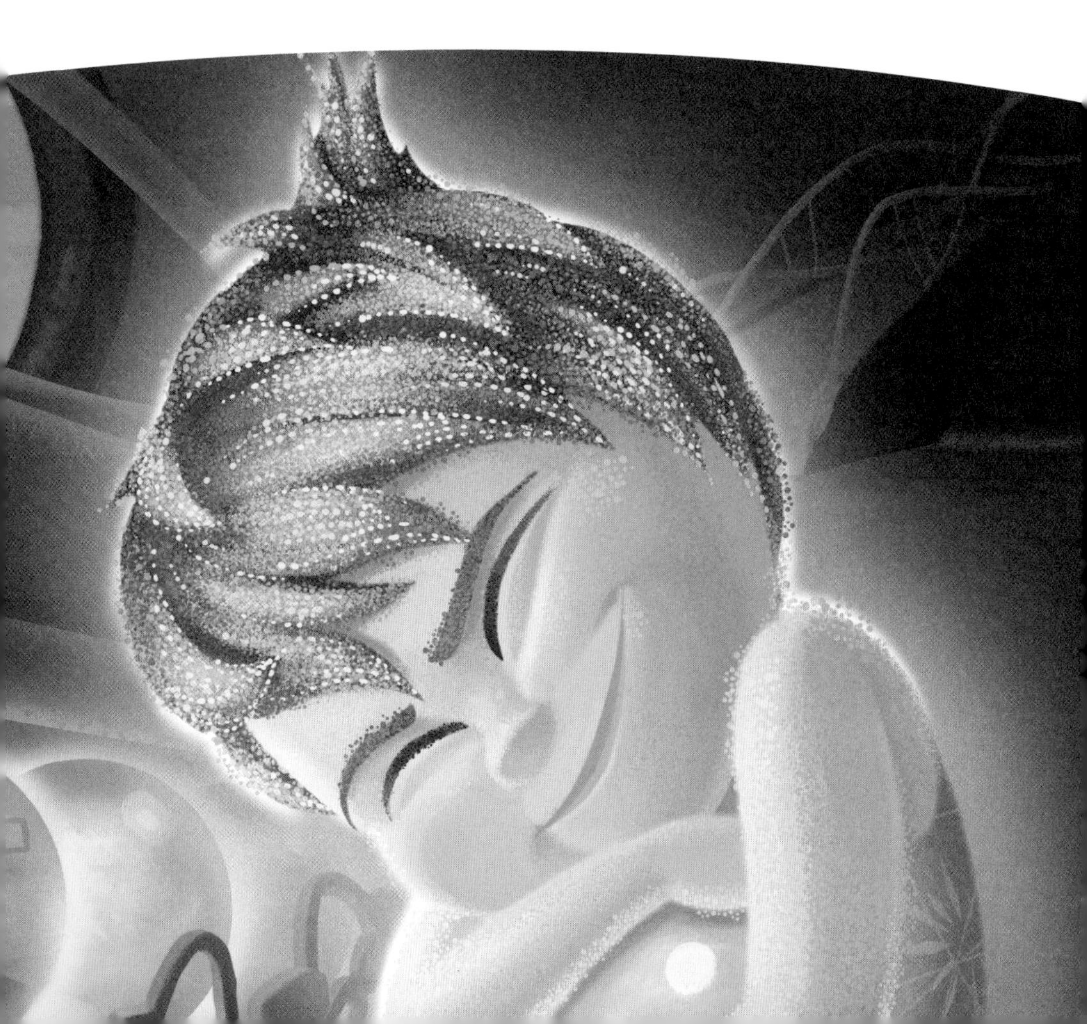

Fear is another Emotion.
He makes sure Riley is safe.
Disgust keeps Riley away
from gross things.

Anger stands up for Riley.
Nobody knows what Sadness does.
Sadness is gloomy and slow.
Riley is always unhappy
when Sadness is in control.

Core memories power
Riley’s Islands of Personality.
There is Family Island,
Honesty Island,
and Hockey Island.

Riley also has
Friendship Island
and Goofball Island.
These islands make Riley
who she is.

The Emotions are shocked when
Riley's family moves
to San Francisco.
They don't know what to do.

Sadness touches a happy memory.
It turns blue
and becomes a sad memory.
Joy must stop Sadness
from touching more
happy memories.

Riley does not like
San Francisco.
The Emotions are worried.
Joy tries to stay positive
and calm them down.

Riley goes to a new school.

She meets her class.

Sadness takes over.

Riley starts to cry.

Joy does not like it

when Riley cries.

Joy tries to stop Sadness.
Joy and Sadness both get sucked out of Headquarters.

Riley's core memories
go with them!
Anger, Fear, and Disgust are
in charge of Headquarters now!

At dinner that night,
Riley is not happy.
She cannot have happy thoughts
without Joy and her core memories.

Riley is angry.
She is rude to her parents.
They send her
to her room.

Goofball Island crumbles
into the Memory Dump.
Nothing comes back
from the Memory Dump.
Joy and Sadness need to get back
to Headquarters quickly!

After dinner,
Riley talks to her friend Meg.
Meg tells her she has a new friend.
Riley gets upset.
Friendship Island crumbles!

When Riley was little,
she had an imaginary friend
named Bing Bong.

Joy and Sadness meet him.
He can help them get back
to Headquarters.

Riley tries out
for the hockey team.
Without her core memories,
she misses the puck and falls!
Hockey Island crumbles!

Bing Bong is sad.
Riley has forgotten about him.
He cries candy.
Sadness talks to Bing Bong.
She makes him feel better.

Anger wants Riley to go back
to her old home
to make new memories.
Riley decides to run away.

Joy, Bing Bong, and Sadness try
to get back to Headquarters.
Joy and Bing Bong fall
into the Memory Dump!
Sadness is alone.

Joy realizes she has been wrong
about Sadness all along.
Riley needs Sadness
to help her feel sad
before she can be happy again.

Joy needs to find Sadness.
Bing Bong helps her get
out of the Memory Dump.

Joy finds Sadness.
They bounce on a trampoline
and get back to Headquarters!

Joy lets Sadness take control.
Sadness helps Riley
feel really sad.
Riley realizes she does not
want to run away.
She goes back to her parents.

Riley tells her parents
that she misses her old home.
Her parents let her know
that it is okay to feel sad.
They hug.

Now all the Emotions work
together in Headquarters
to help Riley.